WE BECAME
JAGUARS

DAVE EGGERS

WOODROW WHITE

chronicle books·san francisco

My grandmother came to visit.

I had met her once before.
She lived far away.
Her hair was very white
and very, very long.

My parents went out and left us alone.

My grandmother got on the carpet and growled.

"Let's be jaguars," she said.

I made the shape of a jaguar.

"No, leaner," she said.
I sucked in my tummy.
"Good," she said.

"Now faster," she said.
I tried to look faster.

"Now fiercer," she said.

I lifted my hands and made them claws.

"Good," she said.

"Now we go."

We went across the front lawn
and into the woods at the end of the cul-de-sac.
I had been in those woods many times,
but I'd never been *through* them.

We went into the night

as jaguars.

As jaguars, we went through.

In the woods we leaped into trees
and scared away squirrels and birds.

"Don't worry," my grandmother said to them.
"We won't eat you. You are too small and gamey!"

She laughed
like great thunder and I laughed
like lesser thunder and we jaguared on.

But when we came upon a rabbit,
my grandmother caught it and ate it
and offered me some.

I didn't want to eat raw rabbit
so I said I was allergic.

My grandmother rolled her jaguar eyes and we jaguared on.

After the woods there was a high hill
and we took it like it was nothing.

At the top of the hill we saw most of the world.

We did not howl because jaguars do not howl.

Jaguars jaguar, so we jaguared on.

Below the hill there was a lake and we went to it
and drank from it.

It looked like silver and tasted like moonlight.
"Mm-mm! That's divine," my grandmother said.

"Mm-mm, that's divine," I said, too, because it was.

"Let's run across this lake," she said.

"Won't we fall in?" I asked.

"Not if we're nimble," she said.

So she ran nimbly and I ran nimbly

and we bounced across like marbles on glass.

On the other side of the lake we lay down
and we rested.

After a few minutes she said, "Let's run some more."

And we ran up a ridge and over a mountain
and across an ocean

and kept running.

We were somewhere in the Himalayas
when I remembered that I had school.
"I should go back pretty soon," I said.

My grandmother looked at me for a while
through her golden jaguar eyes.

"If you say so,"
she said.

We ran back quickly and fiercely and nimbly.
Who knew how much school I had missed?

But it was okay . . .

This book was aided by the input of the Young Editors Project, a program that invites young readers to see manuscripts in-progress. The author and illustrator would like to thank these young editors: At 826 Valencia in San Francisco, California: Jesus, Eduardo, Perla, Aaliyah, Kailyn, Emily, Vanessa, Liliana, Elias, and Jennifer. At Story Factory in Sydney, Australia: Mele, Precilla, Eboney, Grace, Delishar, Travis, Kyle, Jaydon, Izayah, Nick, Mynia, Salesi, Chriseph, Karen, Vai-Jay, Zan, Jack Emily, Jessie, Holly, and Talara

To Mormor and GP. —D. E.

For my grandmothers. —W. W.

Library of Congress Cataloging-in-Publication Data:

Names: Eggers, Dave, author. | White, Woodrow, illustrator.
Title: We became jaguars / written by Dave Eggers ; illustrated by
Woodrow White.
Description: San Francisco : Chronicle Books, 2021. | Audience: Ages 3-5.
| Audience: Grades K-1. | Summary: When Grandma comes to visit, and his
parents leave them alone, the boy's grandmother encourages him to imitate
a jaguar, until completely transformed they venture out into the night,
exploring the world from a new perspective, and with a new freedom—
until it is difficult to distinguish imagination from reality.
Identifiers: LCCN 2019043060 | ISBN 9781452183930 (hardcover)
Subjects: LCSH: Jaguar—Juvenile fiction. | Grandmothers—Juvenile fiction.
| Grandparent and child—Juvenile fiction. | Imagination—Juvenile fiction. |
CYAC: Jaguar—Fiction. | Grandmothers—Fiction. | Imagination—Fiction.
Classification: LCC PZ7.1.E296 We 2020 | DDC 813.54 [E]—dc23
LC record available at https://lccn.loc.gov/2019043060

Manufactured in China.

Design by Jennifer Tolo Pierce.
Typeset in Butler.
The illustrations in this book were rendered in gouache,
acrylic, and digital.

10 9 8 7 6 5 4 3 2 1

Chronicle Books LLC
680 Second Street
San Francisco, California 94107

Chronicle Books—we see things differently. Become part
of our community at www.chroniclekids.com.

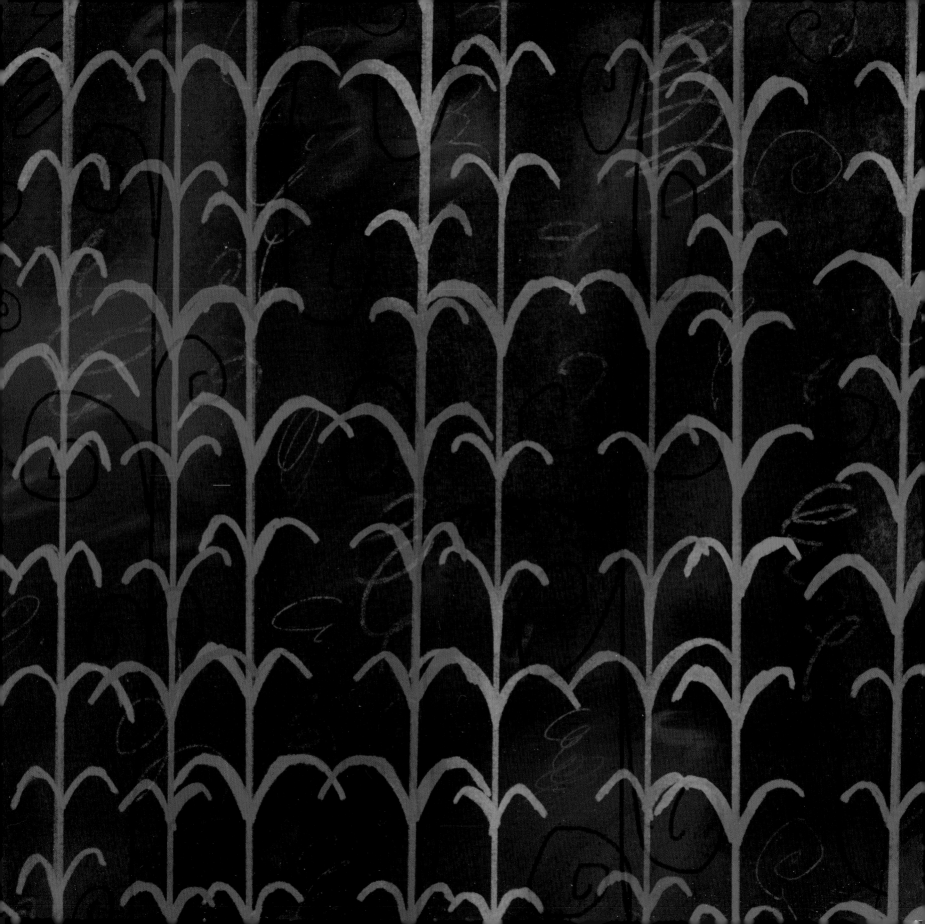